DAY OF DISASTER
Gordon Saves the Day!

Sally Byford

CARLTON
BOOKS

There was great excitement when a space rocket had to be transported across the Allington Suspension Bridge. But it was only half-way over when disaster struck.

The bridge began to shake from side to side and cables began to snap.

Suddenly there was an enormous crash and the whole bridge collapsed.

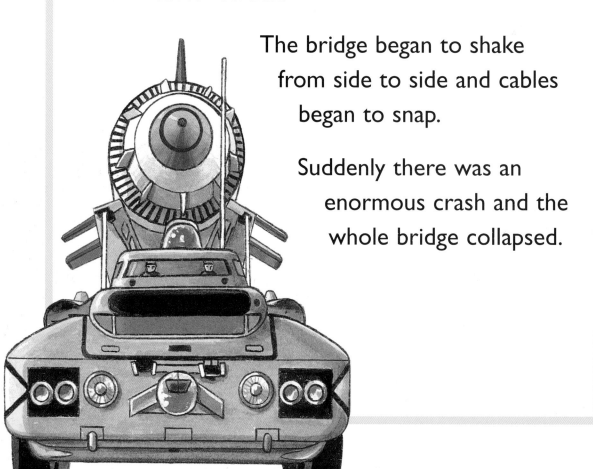

The rocket plunged into the river. Then the automatic launch countdown started. In twelve hours, the rocket would blast off and be blown to pieces, with two men trapped inside the nose cone.

It took the Bridge Controller three hours to establish a radio link with the men. Inside the rocket, Frank and Bill were glad to hear his voice. "Have you called International Rescue?" asked Frank.

"We don't need them," said the Controller. "We have three floating cranes ready to pull you out."

Lady Penelope and Brains had watched the disaster on television and wanted to help. Parker drove them towards the bridge, but they were stopped by a policeman.

"I've got to get to those trapped men," said Brains.

"I'm afraid the way is completely blocked," said the policeman.

"Why don't you cut across the fields and make your own way to the bridge, Brains?" said Lady Penelope.

Brains walked to the bridge and managed to get into the control room. "Your equipment looks too old for a job like this," he said. "You'd better call International Rescue."

The Controller was very cross. "Watch this troublemaker," he told his assistant. "Don't let him near the bridge."

Brains quietly contacted John Tracy on his watch radio. "I've got a job for you," he said.

John contacted his father on the two-way TV.

"I've just heard from Brains. He says the
equipment at Allington Bridge is very old.
And there are only seven hours left
before the rocket blasts off. They need
our help."

"OK, John," said Jeff. "Tell Brains we'll
be there as soon as we can. Scott, take
Thunderbird 1 and check out what's
happening. Gordon and Virgil,
take Thunderbirds 2 and 4.
Good luck, boys."

Inside the rocket, Frank and Bill watched the clock. There were five hours left when the Controller called again.

"We're ready," he said.

The huge cranes struggled to pull the rocket out, but it wouldn't move. One by one, the cranes sank into the river. The Controller's plan had failed.

"Only International Rescue can save us now," he said.

"They're already on their way," said Brains.

It wasn't long before Scott reached the bridge. "It looks pretty bad, father," he said. "I can't do anything until Virgil and Gordon arrive."

Thunderbird 2 got there an hour later. Virgil quickly dropped the pod into the water and released Gordon in Thunderbird 4.

Gordon investigated under water. He saw that the rocket was completely surrounded by rubble from the broken bridge. "It's a real mess down here," he told Brains.

Brains asked Virgil to clear the rubble away from the rocket using Thunderbird 2's giant grabs. Virgil worked as quickly as he could, but he didn't have much time left.

Inside the rocket, Frank and Bill had no idea what was happening.

"There are only fifteen minutes left," said Frank. "They can't help us now."

Brains contacted Gordon again. "Is the nose cone clear yet?" he asked.

"No, it's not," said Gordon. "We'll never make it in time."

Brains thought hard. "Try using the missiles,"
he said.

So Gordon fired at the rubble. Inside, Frank and
Bill heard the explosions.

"They're trying to blow us to pieces," said Frank.

"We're going to be blown up anyway," said Bill.
"Look at the time!" There were only
eight minutes left.

The missiles cleared the rubble. Then Gordon drove Thunderbird 4 into the nose cone at top speed. The cone broke free from the rest of the rocket and floated to the top of the river.

There were now five minutes to lift-off. Virgil lowered the claw from Thunderbird 2 and held the nose cone tightly. He lifted it out of the water and carried it to dry land.

Frank and Bill couldn't believe their luck. "We're out of the river," cried Bill. "And there's still half a minute to go!"

BILL

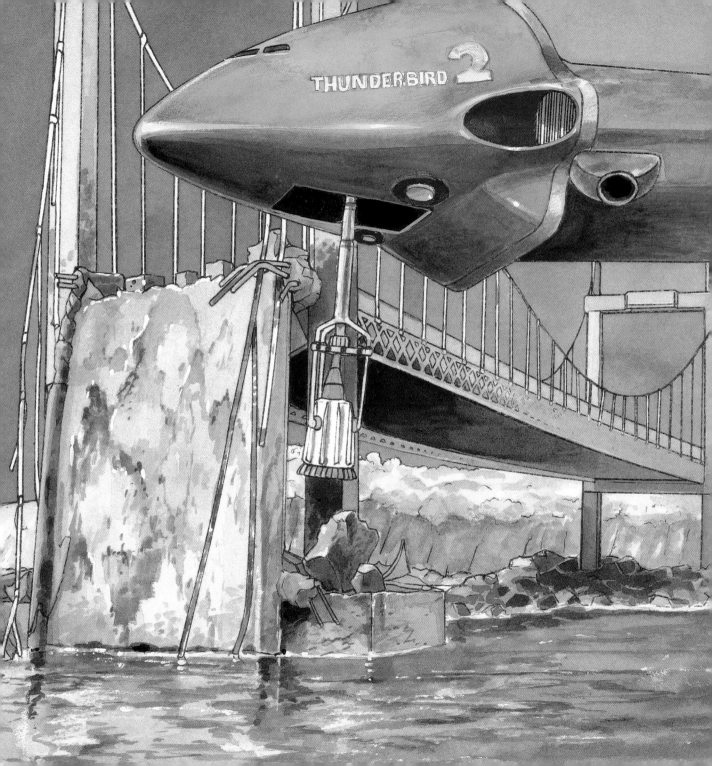

Seconds later, the countdown was over. The rocket blasted up into the sky. As everyone watched, it slowed down, started to fall and then exploded in a ball of flames.

"International Rescue has done it!" said the Controller.

Brains danced around the room feeling very happy.

It was the end of a disastrous day for Allington Suspension Bridge, but thanks to International Rescue Frank and Bill were safe at last.

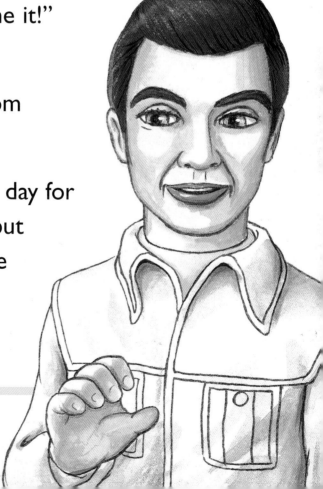

THIS IS A CARLTON BOOK

Published by Carlton Books Limited 2000
20 Mortimer Street
London W1N 7RD

2 4 6 8 10 9 7 5 3 1

A CIP catalogue for this book is available from the British Library.

ISBN 1 84222 099 3

Illustrations by County Studio
Language consultant: Betty Root, formerly director of
Reading Centre, The University of Reading
Project editor: Lesley Levene
Production: Garry Lewis

Printed in Singapore